Usborne Beginners

Dinosaurs

Stephanie Turnbull
Designed by Zöe Wray
Illustrated by Tetsuo Kushii

Additional illustrations by Uwe Mayer

Dinosaur consultant: Dr Neil D. L. Clark, Hunterian Museum, University of Glasgow

Reading consultant: Alison Kelly, University of Surrey Roehampton

Contents

Long, long ago

Dinosaurs were animals that lived millions of years ago, long before there were any people.

This is an Apatosaurus family.

There were thousands of different dinosaurs.

What is a dinosaur?

A dinosaur is a type of reptile.
Reptiles are animals with scaly skin,
like crocodiles and lizards.

This dinosaur is an Allosaurus.

Scaly skin

Thick, powerful tail

Some dinosaurs
lived for more
than 100 years.

4

Long snout

Sharp claws

Slim, light dinosaurs ran quickly on two legs.

Heavy dinosaurs plodded slowly on four legs.

Dinosaur world

When dinosaurs lived, the world had many more forests, deserts and rivers than today.

These dinosaurs are Anatotitans. They lived in forests and drank from rivers.

It was much hotter in dinosaur times than it is now.

There were other animals too. Reptiles with big, flapping wings flew through the air.

All kinds of strange-looking reptiles lived in rivers and seas.

There were also lots of insects and small animals like those you see today.

7

Big and small

Some dinosaurs were the biggest land animals ever. Others were very small.

This enormous dinosaur is called Brachiosaurus. It was heavier than 15 elephants.

A dinosaur called Microraptor was smaller than a hen.

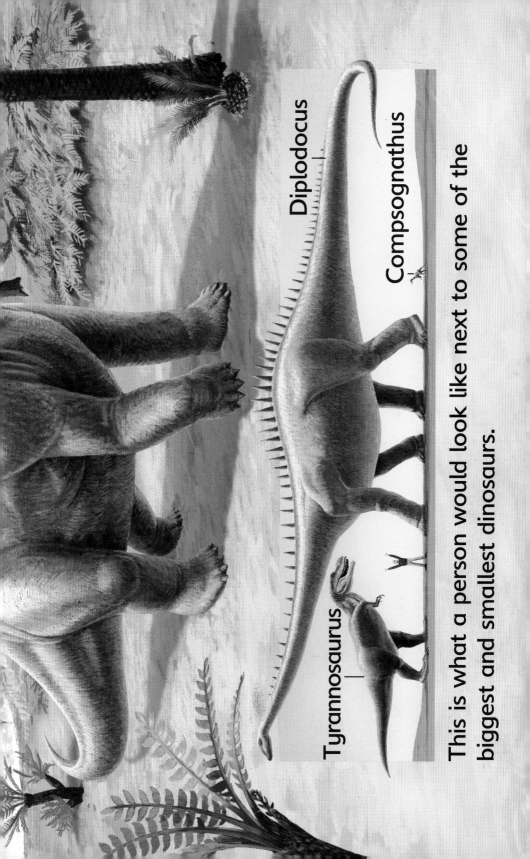

Diplodocus

Compsognathus

Tyrannosaurus

This is what a person would look like next to some of the biggest and smallest dinosaurs.

Plant munchers

Lots of dinosaurs ate plants. They spent all day feeding on tasty leaves.

Stegosaurus looked big and scary, but it only ate plants.

It had a hard mouth like a beak for biting off leaves.

Dinosaurs with long necks could reach high branches.

They could also stretch out and grab plants from far away.

This skull belonged to a Psittacosaurus. Its bony beak sliced easily through stalks.

Some plant-eaters had thousands of teeth for grinding leaves and twigs.

Fierce hunters

Some dinosaurs were meat-eaters.
They ate lizards, snakes and other animals.
They often attacked dinosaurs too.

Meat-eaters such as Troodons
were always on the lookout
for animals to catch.

Many meat-eaters
had special
jaws that
opened
extra-wide.

Some of the most dangerous dinosaurs were very small. They hunted in groups.

They were fast movers, so they could easily catch clumsy plant-eaters.

The hunters pounced on their prey and sank their sharp teeth into it.

Killer claws

Dinosaurs that ate meat had long, sharp claws on their hands and feet.

This huge, curved claw belonged to a Baryonyx.

Baryonyx used its claws to spike fish in the water.

Velociraptor walked with its big claws up, to keep them sharp.

It flicked the claws forward to slash an enemy in a fight.

Allosaurus had three razor-sharp claws on each hand.

A dinosaur called Deinocheirus had claws that were almost as long as your arm.

Dinosaur king

Tyrannosaurus was one of the biggest, most terrifying dinosaurs. It could have eaten you in one mouthful.

Tyrannosaurus prowled through the forest.

It rushed at victims with its enormous mouth wide open.

It had about 50 long, pointed teeth that could crunch bones.

Tyrannosaurus was so fierce that no animal dared to steal its food.

Tyrannosaurus was huge, but its arms were tiny. No one knows why they were so small.

Sticking together

Many plant-eating dinosaurs lived in large groups, or herds.

They protected each other by looking out for enemies.

These dinosaurs are hadrosaurs. Some hadrosaurs had big, hollow horns on their heads.

Hadrosaurs could blow air up through their horn.

This made a honking sound to warn other hadrosaurs of danger.

Herds of big dinosaurs probably left trampled trees and plants behind them.

Stay away!

Some dinosaurs had ways of protecting themselves from enemies.

Euoplocephalus had a heavy, bony club on its tail for swinging at enemies.

Its body was covered in hard plates that were too thick to bite through.

Triceratops had a bony frill that made it look big and fierce.

Albertosaurus

It could also stab enemies with its long, pointed horns.

Euoplocephalus

A few dinosaurs had extra-thick skulls. They butted each other with them.

Eggs and babies

Baby dinosaurs hatched out of eggs.

1. A mother dinosaur made a nest and laid about 20 eggs.

2. She covered the eggs with leaves to keep them warm.

3. A baby made a hole in its egg and wiggled out.

4. It left the nest and started to look for food.

Some dinosaurs looked after their babies. They made sure that other dinosaurs didn't eat them.

Dinosaur eggs could be small and round or long and thin.

Where did they go?

Dinosaurs lived for millions of years but then they suddenly died out. No one is sure why.

Many scientists think that a big space rock crashed into Earth.

The crash made the ground tremble and crack. Huge fires started.

Dust filled the air so that it was too dark and cold for dinosaurs to live.

Lots of volcanoes
erupted too. This killed
off plants, so dinosaurs
had nothing to eat.

Some other animals
didn't die. Perhaps
they hid until it
was safe to come
out again.

Buried bones

Scientists find dinosaur bones in the ground. The bones have turned to stone and are called fossils.

1. A dinosaur died. Soon only its skeleton was left.

2. It was covered in mud. Slowly, the mud turned into rock.

3. After many years, the bones turned into fossils.

4. When the rock wears away, the fossils are left.

This fossil hunter has discovered the foot of a huge Jobaria dinosaur.

He cleans soil off the bones with a brush.

Dinosaur fossils are found all the time. There might be some in the ground beneath you!

Dino detectives

If scientists find a lot of bones from one dinosaur, they try to put them together.

They work out where each bone should go. It's like doing a giant jigsaw puzzle.

Scientists used to think dinosaurs were tall, with bent tails.

Now they know that dinosaurs held their tails out straight.

This is a Triceratops.
Its bones are held in
place with metal rods.

No one knows
what dinosaur skin
looked like. Perhaps
it was covered in
spots or stripes!

Glossary of dinosaur words

Here are some of the words in this book you might not know. This page tells you what they mean.

 scaly - skin that is covered in lots of tiny, thin plates.

 snout - an animal's nose and mouth. Most dinosaurs had long, thin snouts.

 claw - a curved, sharp spike on the end of an animal's finger or toe.

 prey - an animal that is hunted by other animals to eat.

 herd - a group of animals that live and feed together.

 hatch - break out of an egg. All dinosaurs hatched from eggs.

 fossil - a bone or other part of an animal that has turned into stone.